For Rotem Moscovich
For her year-round help
and inestimable guidance

And for Julia Sooy
With thanks and gratitude

—A.M.M. and L.G.

For Mom and Dad,
thanks for all the Christmas memories

—B.H.

Text copyright © 2016 by Ann M. Martin and Laura Godwin
Illustrations copyright © 2016 by Brett Helquist

First Edition, September 2016
10 9 8 7 6 5 4 3 2 1
FAC-029191-16198

Printed in Malaysia

Library of Congress Cataloging-in-Publication Data
Names: Martin, Ann M., 1955- author. | Godwin, Laura, author. | Helquist, Brett, illustrator.
Title: The doll people's Christmas / by Ann M. Martin and Laura Godwin ; illustrated by Brett Helquist.
Description: First edition. | Los Angeles ; New York : Disney-Hyperion, 2016. | Summary: Things go awry when Annabelle, a fragile, timid porcelain doll who lives in a Victorian dollhouse, tries to share some of her Christmas traditions with best friend Tiffany, a sturdy, adventurous plastic doll who lives in a modern dollhouse.
Identifiers: LCCN 2015039664| ISBN 9781484723395 (hardback) | ISBN 1484723392
Subjects: | CYAC: Dolls—Fiction. | Dollhouses—Fiction. | Christmas—Fiction. | BISAC: JUVENILE FICTION / Holidays & Celebrations / Christmas & Advent. | JUVENILE FICTION / Toys, Dolls, Puppets. | JUVENILE FICTION / Family / General (see also headings under Social Issues).
Classification: LCC PZ7.M3567585 Ds 2016 | DDC [E] —dc23
LC record available at http://lccn.loc.gov/2015039664

Reinforced binding
Visit www.DisneyBooks.com

THE DOLL PEOPLE'S CHRISTMAS

WRITTEN BY **ANN M. MARTIN** *and* **LAURA GODWIN**

ILLUSTRATED BY **BRETT HELQUIST**

DISNEP • HYPERION

LOS ANGELES   NEW YORK

In an old Victorian dollhouse in the corner of
Kate Palmer's room lived Annabelle Doll and her old
Victorian family—Mama, Papa, Uncle Doll, Auntie
Sarah, Bobby, Baby Betsy, and Nanny, who was the
nanny to the three Doll children.

Annabelle was fragile and timid, and very relieved
that Kate kept her room and the Dolls' house tidy and
orderly. Annabelle liked her bed just so and her house
just so and her life just so.

Down the hall, in the room belonging to Kate's little sister Nora, was a modern dollhouse made of plastic, where Tiffany Funcraft lived with her modern plastic family—Mom, Dad, Bailey, and Baby Britney.

Tiffany was sturdy and adventurous. She was grateful that Nora was wild and noisy, and that she kept her room and the Funcrafts' house a mess.

"Messy, messy, messy!" Tiffany would exclaim. "Just the way I like things."

Annabelle and Tiffany were different—and they were best friends. They were both interested in the world of the humans, but understood what it meant to lead lives that must be kept secret.

"No moving about when a human might see you," the adults would remind them.

Nighttime was the best time because the humans were asleep. The dolls didn't have to be quite so careful.

There was just one problem: The Captain, who was not a captain at all but a cat. The Captain caused trouble day and night.

Every year, Annabelle looked forward to Christmas. This year the Funcrafts, who were new dolls, would celebrate the holiday for the very first time.

"I'm going to show Tiffany the perfect Christmas," Annabelle said to Auntie Sarah.

Annabelle was so very old that she had celebrated
more than one hundred Christmases in the Dolls'
house, so she knew what made Christmas perfect:
singing carols with her family, admiring the presents,
watching Kate decorate the rooms just so, and waiting to
see the final ornament—the angel on the top of the tree.

December fifteenth was decorating day. Down from the Palmers' attic came the box of decorations for Annabelle's house —the wreath for the door, the wrapped packages, the cards and candies and gingerbread cookies. Kate unwrapped each item and set it in its familiar spot.

"I wish Tiffany could see this," Annabelle whispered.

Mama Doll gave her a stern look, and Annabelle closed her mouth.

At last Kate unwrapped . . .

. . . the tree!

Time for tinsel, Annabelle thought. *Time for lights. Time for my favorite ornament of all.*

Kate
unwrapped
the
angel.

It wasn't her fault that she dropped it. It was just one of those things that happens.

Annabelle cried silently. Kate cried loudly. "Don't worry," Grandma Katherine said. "Your mother is out shopping right now. She can buy another angel."

It won't be the same, thought Annabelle.

"It won't be the same," said Kate.

It was even worse than Annabelle had imagined.

"I'm sorry," said Kate's mother, when she came home. "They were out of angels."

But there's nothing for the top of the tree, thought Annabelle.

"But there's nothing for the top of the tree," wailed Kate.

That was when Annabelle knew Christmas was ruined.

That night Annabelle glared at the tree. "It isn't right!" she exclaimed to Tiffany. "We're supposed to have an angel on the tree."
"Why?"
"Because we always do."

"Annabelle," said Mama gently, "sometimes things change."
But Annabelle didn't want anything about her perfect Christmas
to change.

On December twenty-fourth something unexpected happened.

"Time for a Christmas Eve visit!" said Nora. She snuck into

Kate's room with the Funcrafts and eight plastic cows.

A Christmas Eve visit? Perfect! thought Annabelle.

But not one thing about the visit was perfect.

Kate was not happy to see what her sister had done.

"Nora! How many times have I told you to leave my dollhouse alone? Put everything back right now."

"No," said Nora.

"Yes," said Kate. She gathered up the cows.

"Wait," said Nora. "I have an idea." She began to whisper to her sister.

The next thing Annabelle knew, she was clasped in Kate's hand.

Annabelle peered through Kate's
fingers. She had never left her house
at Christmastime before.

Lights everywhere!

Decorations everywhere!

The Palmers' house sparkled and
twinkled. Annabelle's heart beat
faster. The dolls were on a Christmas
adventure.

Annabelle felt herself being placed gently on the floor.
"We'll be right back, dollies," called Kate.

Annabelle slid her eyes to the right and left. She
saw a gingerbread house. She saw cards and cookies and
candies. She saw an impossibly tall tree with an angel—
a proper angel—on top.

"*They* have an angel," Annabelle whispered crossly to
Tiffany. "A perfect, not-messed-up Christmas tree with
an *angel* on top."

Kate and Nora returned with a basket of art supplies. They fashioned a beard for Papa Doll and gave him a candy cane for a staff. They taped paper wings to Mom Funcraft and Auntie Sarah and Annabelle. They stuck cotton balls to the rest of the dolls. "So many angels and so many sheep!" said Nora.

"You're going to stay here, dolls," added Kate, "so you can wake up in the crèche on Christmas morning."

Annabelle stared around the stable in despair. She was going to miss Christmas in the dollhouse for the first time in her very long life.

Darkness fell. Annabelle could feel the excitement in Kate's house.

"See you on Christmas," Kate whispered to her dolls.

"This is wrong!" Annabelle said when the house was quiet. "Completely and entirely wrong. How can I show you the perfect Christmas now?"

"We can see Christmas right here," replied Tiffany. "Let's explore."

Annabelle and Tiffany crept around the room, examining the cookies for Santa and poking at the presents under the tree.

"Too bad these presents aren't for us," said Tiffany.

"What's that noise?" whispered Annabelle suddenly.

Something large and furry swiped at Annabelle.

The Captain.

"Run!" called Tiffany, and she scooted under the couch.

Annabelle ran, but The Captain's paw caught her dress and sent her skidding across the floor.

The Captain leaped in the air. He swatted at the ornaments on the tree. Then he flew to the back of the couch and perched there, eyes wide and tail twitching.

Annabelle, leaning against a present under the tree, watched The Captain and dared not move. She looked up, up, up through the green branches and shimmering ornaments.

Across the room, Annabelle's family and her friends gathered nervously outside the stable. Uncle Doll wrung his hands.

Into the silence came a sound, different from the one before. A small thump on the roof. The Captain jumped to the floor and galloped from the room. Annabelle and Tiffany ran to each other, clasped hands, and scurried back to the crèche.

Mama Doll pulled Annabelle close.

Annabelle heard rustling behind her. She heard
the branches of the Christmas tree swishing. Then the
noises stopped, and the house grew quiet again.

Annabelle dared to turn around.

"Tiffany! The stockings are full."

"And there's one for you."

"With a star for our tree," whispered Annabelle.

"But you wanted an angel," said Tiffany. "An angel to make your Christmas perfect."

Annabelle thought about the cows on the roof and the Christmas visit gone wrong. She thought about the broken angel and The Captain and spending the night in the Palmers' living room.

Then she thought about the crèche and the stuffed stockings and spending Christmas Eve with her best friend.

"I think," said Annabelle,
"that I had the perfect Christmas after all."